RENEE BEAUREGARD LUTE

Winicker
Wallace

Winicker and the Christmas Visit

ILLUSTRATED BY LAURA HORTON

An Imprint of Magic Wagon
abdopublishing.com

For Maddie, Simon, and Cecily, who inspire me, for Zach, who encourages me, and for my mom, who's told even her hair stylist about Winicker. —RL

To my brother Jesse – who still keeps some of my embarrassingly bad drawings. —LH

abdopublishing.com

Published by Magic Wagon, a division of ABDO, PO Box 398166, Minneapolis, Minnesota 55439. Copyright © 2018 by Abdo Consulting Group, Inc. International copyrights reserved in all countries. No part of this book may be reproduced in any form without written permission from the publisher. Calico™ is a trademark and logo of Magic Wagon.

Printed in the United States of America, North Mankato, Minnesota.
102017
012018

 THIS BOOK CONTAINS RECYCLED MATERIALS

Written by Renee Beauregard Lute
Illustrated by Laura Horton
Edited by Heidi M.D. Elston
Art Directed by Laura Mitchell

Publisher's Cataloging-in-Publication Data

Names: Lute, Renee Beauregard, author. | Horton, Laura, illustrator.
Title: Winicker and the Christmas visit / by Renee Beauregard Lute; illustrated by Laura Horton.
Description: Minneapolis, Minnesota : Magic Wagon, 2018. | Series: Winicker Wallace
Summary: Winicker Wallace's best friend, Roxanne, is going to spend Christmas Eve in Paris, and Winicker is beyond thrilled. When Roxanne arrives in Paris, however, she doesn't want to do all of the traditional Christmas things Winicker had planned. She wants to see the sights of Paris! When Winicker and Roxanne find themselves celebrating Christmas in a way neither of them expected, they discover they haven't grown so far apart after all.
Identifiers: LCCN 2017946544 | ISBN 9781532130502 (lib.bdg.) | ISBN 9781532131103 (ebook) | ISBN 9781532131400 (Read-to-me ebook)
Subjects: LCSH: Christmas--Juvenile fiction. | Friendship in children--Juvenile fiction. | Friendly visiting--Juvenile fiction. | Humorous Stories--Juvenile fiction.
Classification: DDC [FIC]--dc23
LC record available at https://lccn.loc.gov/2017946544

Things to Do with Roxanne in Paris

Dear Reader,

I don't know your actual real name, so just pretend your name is in the place where I wrote "Reader."

There are some French and Spanish words in this book, because this book takes place in Paris and there are Spanish-speaking characters. When you see a French or Spanish word that you don't know, just flip to the back of the book! There is a glossary back there that will tell you what *bonjour* and *merci* mean, and lots of other words, too.

I know what you are thinking. "Wow, thank you so much! That is really helpful."

You're welcome. I hope you enjoy this very amazing and hilarious story.

Love,

Winicker

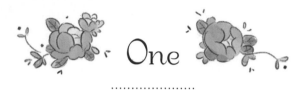

One

MAKE THOSE GREEN FROSTING COOKIES WITH SILVER BALLS

Tomorrow is going to be the best day ever. Tomorrow, my best friend Roxanne is flying from Three Rivers, Massachusetts, to visit me in Paris! She is staying here for a whole week! She is coming for Christmas with her grandmother, Granny Bee.

Granny Bee is short for Granny Becky, which is short for Granny Rebecca. Granny Bee is my Grandma Balthazar's best friend in the whole world.

I have two best friends, and the second one is Mirabel Plouffe, my FBFANDN (French best friend and next door neighbor). Mirabel Plouffe is going to meet Roxanne for the first time. They will probably become best friends too.

But maybe not quite as best friends as me and Roxanne. And less best than me and Mirabel Plouffe. But still best friends.

And we could call ourselves the Tremendous Three. *Tremendous* means "great," which is what we will be.

"Winicker, you look just as excited as I feel!" Grandma Balthazar says. We are all sitting at the kitchen table: me, Grandma Balthazar, Mom, Dad, and my baby brother, Walter, in Mom's arms. We're all having cinnamon and brown sugar oatmeal with raisins for breakfast. Except Walter, because he can only have milk. He's a new baby. New babies get milk.

It is our last breakfast before I am on Christmas break from school! It is our last breakfast before Roxanne gets here!

"I am so excited!" I say. "We're going to do all of the Christmas stuff we used to do in Three Rivers. We're going to decorate cookies with

weird green frosting and little silver balls. And speaking of silver, I can't wait for Roxanne to see my hair!"

My silver hair is from Grandma Balthazar's hair dye. It looks magnificent, which is another word for tremendous.

"We're going to watch Christmas movies and make a gingerbread house," I say. "And we'll listen to Christmas music in our pajamas! I can't wait until she gets here tomorrow!"

"Those things sound like a lot of fun," says Dad. He has a couple spots of oatmeal and a raisin down the front of his flannel shirt. "But remember, Winicker," he says, "Roxanne's never been to Paris before. She'll probably want to get out and see the sights, too."

Grandma Balthazar breathes in really deeply. That means she is going to say something like an old movie star would say in an old black-and-white movie. Her silver hair sparkles under the kitchen lights. "The sights! The sounds! The smells!" She claps her hands together. "I can't wait to show Bee and Roxanne around my beautiful city!"

I mush my oatmeal around the bowl a little with my spoon. "Okay, but remember they're here for Christmas. So we're going to mostly do all of the Christmas things we used to do in Three Rivers."

Mom wipes milk off of Walter's face and looks at Dad. Then she looks at Grandma Balthazar. Then she looks at me. "Honey, let's make plans *with* Roxanne and Granny Bee. Not *for* them. No matter what you do with Roxanne, it's going to be a lot of fun. Just don't get too attached to a list or schedule. Roxanne may not want to do everything on your list."

I put down my spoon. "Trust me, I know Roxanne. She will."

At my desk in room 3A at La Petite École Internationale de Paris, I can't concentrate on anything Mademoiselle Bennett is saying. She is pointing at a colorful map of France. There are pictures of cows and cheese and wheat all over it.

"Voici!" says Mademoiselle Bennett. "Agriculture in France. France is one of the largest exporters . . ."

"Psst, Mirabel Plouffe," I say. I lean forward. In room 3A, all of the desks are pushed together in groups of four. I share my desk cluster with Mirabel Plouffe, awful Maizy Durand, and a new girl named Amal Aziz. Amal Aziz draws tiny pictures at the top of all of her homework.

Mirabel Plouffe leans forward. "Winicker, we should pay attention. This is our last chance to learn anything before it is the holidays!"

I ignore her.

"My other best friend Roxanne is coming tomorrow," I say.

"Yes, I know," Mirabel Plouffe whispers.

"We all know," says awful Maizy Durand.

I ignore Maizy Durand, too.

"We're going to do all of the fun Christmas stuff we used to do in Three Rivers," I say to Mirabel Plouffe. "You can come over and do it all with us! You've probably never made green frosting cookies with silver balls on them before."

"Those sound dis-gus-ting," says awful Maizy Durand.

"Those sound delicious," says Amal Aziz. Amal Aziz's parents don't let her have very much sugar. They own a health food and vegan footwear store in Paris called La Nourriture.

"We're going to watch a bunch of Christmas movies in our pajamas," I say.

"That sounds boring," says awful Maizy Durand.

"Mm-hmm," says Mirabel Plouffe. She is trying to look past me so she can see Mademoiselle

Bennett and the agriculture map.

Amal Aziz doesn't say anything. She is drawing pictures of cookies all over a page in her notebook.

"And we're going to—"

"Winicker Wallace, are you listening?" Mademoiselle Bennett is pointing at a picture of grapes, but she is looking at me.

"Yes, Mademoiselle," I say. "Grapes."

Mademoiselle Bennett looks kind of suspicious, but she turns back to the map. "There are many breeds of French cattle, including . . ."

"Psst, Mirabel Plouffe," I say.

Mirabel Plouffe finally looks at me. "Winicker, I know you are very excited that Roxanne is coming tomorrow. But perhaps you should also plan to do some new things with Roxanne. She is coming to Paris for the very first time! She will want to see all of the wonderful Parisian things in our city. She will want to eat les macarons and buttery sablés. She will want to see the towers of cream puffs covered in chocolate in the bakery windows—"

Amal Aziz does a very loud sigh. She has drawn a person made out of cookies in her notebook. He has chocolate chips for eyes.

"Mirabel Plouffe," I say, "Trust me. Roxanne is going to want to do all of the usual Three Rivers Christmas things."

"But Winicker, Paris is—"

"Paris is Paris," I say. "But tradition is tradition!"

"Winicker Wallace," says Mademoiselle Bennett. "Please tell me. What are the three main agricultural exports in France? We just went over them. Were you listening?"

"I don't know," I say. "Green frosting cookies with silver balls?"

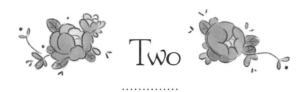

Two

She's here! Roxanne is here in Paris! She is on her way to my apartment with Granny Bee. They are taking a taxi from the airport.

I hope she looks exactly the same way she did the last time I saw her. I hope she brought her same teddy bear, Osito. I hope she brought her same pajamas with dogs wearing wigs all over them.

Grandma Balthazar and I are sitting at the kitchen table. She is looking into her cup of black coffee and pretending to be calm. But I can tell she is excited. Her high-heeled shoes are dancing under the table.

A black car pulls up outside of our apartment. The light on top says Taxi Parisien. Roxanne!

"They're here!" I say.

Grandma Balthazar and I jump up from the table and rush outside into the cold air. We run to the taxi, and a backseat door swings open.

"It's Rox—" I start to say. I only start to say it, because it isn't Roxanne. It's a man. A man with a beard and wearing a long orange robe and a gold crown with sparkly blue stones in it.

The man sticks his head and crown out of the taxi. "Am I in the right place?" The man has a British accent. "Is this Gaia's flat? Are Megan and everyone inside? I had to rush from work, so I changed in the car. I hate to be late for these things. Do you know if the actual live sheep will be at rehearsal? I have an allergy, so I'll need to take my medicine."

I look at Grandma Balthazar. Normally, I would be very interested in this person and his sparkly crown. And I would be especially interested in the sheep. How can you be allergic to sheep? But today I'm not interested in anything except seeing my friend Roxanne.

"I'm sorry, sir," says Grandma Balthazar. "I'm afraid you must have the wrong address."

"Yeah," I say. "There are no sheep here."

The man looks kind of disappointed. I notice he is holding a box in his lap. A very shiny box, with sparkly blue stones all over it, just like the ones in his crown.

Well, okay. I'm a little interested.

"What's in that box?" I ask.

The man looks down at the box. "Well, I'm not really sure. Gold, I think. Or frankincense. Myrrh, maybe? I'm one of the Magi in a nativity tableau vivant. Today is our dress rehearsal. We're performing Monday at the Christmas market on the Champs-Élysées."

"Oh," I say. "Like a Christmas pageant."

The man sighs. "No, it's a tableau vivant. A living picture. We don't move or talk."

"You just stand there?" I ask.

"Well, yes," he says. "I kneel, but some of us stand there. The point is to be as quiet and still as a fake nativity scene."

"Why don't they just get a fake nativity scene?" I ask. "Instead of getting real people to pretend to be a fake nativity scene?"

The man looks a little sad. "I don't know. I hadn't thought about that."

"Well," Grandma Balthazar says, "I'm sure it's wonderful to look at. Maybe we'll swing by the Christmas market on Monday."

The man straightens his crown. "Yeah?" he says. "Well, I'd better get to rehearsal, wherever it is. Cheers!" He shuts his door.

A second later, another black taxi pulls up in the same spot. My stomach gets a fluttery kind of feeling. The windows are too dark to see inside.

"Do you think it's Bee and Roxanne," says Grandma Balthazar, "or a nativity shepherd?"

The back door flings open, and Roxanne jumps out! "Winicker Wallace!" she yells.

"Roxanne Rodríguez!" I yell back.

She wraps me up in the best hug in the whole world. Nothing has changed. Roxanne is the same. Roxanne's hugs are the same. And Roxanne's—. Wait. Roxanne's ears are not the same.

I pull back and look closer. There are tiny gold earrings in Roxanne's ears!

"Roxanne! You got your ears pierced!" I feel excited for her because I'm not allowed to get my ears pierced. Even though I begged all three of the grown-ups in my apartment. Even though I begged them separately so they would not know the other grown-ups had already said no.

But I also get kind of a small bad feeling inside, because she didn't tell me she got her ears pierced. And Roxanne tells me everything. And I tell Roxanne everything! Why didn't she tell me she got her ears pierced?

"Ohh, yeah!" Roxanne touches her earlobes. "I got them pierced a few weeks ago. And your silver hair looks awesome! I'm in Paris, Winicker!" She grabs me for another big hug.

I try to forget about the earrings. I try to forget about the fact that she didn't tell me about

getting her ears pierced, even though I told her I dyed my hair silver.

"You're in Paris!" I say. We jump up and down and keep hugging. "And it's Christmas! And we're going to do all of the Christmas stuff we always used to do in Three Rivers!"

Roxanne laughs. We stop jumping and hugging. "I hope not! We're in the City of Light! I want to see all kinds of new stuff!"

I get another small bad feeling inside. "Well, we'll do some of the usual Three Rivers Christmas stuff," I say. "And anyway, it's the City of Love."

Grandma Balthazar is hugging Granny Bee a couple of feet away. There are two big, purple suitcases on the sidewalk next to them.

"Nope," says Roxanne. "It's the City of Light." She pulls a small book out of her pocket and waggles it back and forth. There is a picture of the Eiffel Tower on the front. I hope she doesn't want to go to the Eiffel Tower. I only went to the Eiffel Tower once, and I did not have a fun time.

"I read this travel guide three times. It says it's the City of Light. I can't wait to see everything!"

I don't like the way any of this sounds. And I'm pretty sure it's the City of Love. I don't care what an old travel guide says. I live here.

It starts to rain. I shiver a little. "Let's go inside," I say. "We're going to get all wet. It rains a lot here."

"Yeah, I know," Roxanne says. She waggles her travel guide again and then shoves it back into her pocket. "The book says to pack a raincoat."

Ugh. The book again.

We all hurry through the courtyard to my front door. Grandma Balthazar and Granny Bee don't hurry as fast as me and Roxanne. They are old and have to roll big, purple suitcases.

Mom and Dad fling open the door as soon as we reach it.

"Bee! Roxanne!" Mom says. She is smiling a huge smile. But then she frowns. "Winicker, why aren't you helping with the suitcases?"

"Ugg! Ugg!" Walter cries from the kitchen. He doesn't ever say "waaah" like other babies.

"Alice!" Granny Bee rushes up to Mom and hugs her tight, rocking back and forth.

"Ugg!" Walter yells again.

Granny Bee claps her hands together.

"El bebé!" She brushes past Mom and goes inside to see Walter. Mom follows her. People are like that with babies. I'm used to it by now.

Roxanne and Granny Bee and I sit down around the kitchen table.

"Whew!" says Roxanne. "That plane ride was no joke. I'm tired, and my butt hurts."

"Roxanne!" says Granny Bee. "We're guests. And we're in Paris. Don't say 'my butt hurts!'"

"Sorry, sorry. Jeez," says Roxanne. "I mean my derrière hurts."

Roxanne and I both laugh. We look at Granny Bee. Granny Bee looks so not-laughing that it makes us laugh all over again.

"You must be tired!" says Grandma Balthazar. She sits down at the table, too. "Why don't we all have a nice evening in tonight? I can make my famous roasted chicken, and we can all watch a Christmas movie in our pajamas. Just like the old days in Three Rivers." She winks at me.

I love Grandma Balthazar a lot. She knows just what to say, sometimes. She knows that watching a movie in our pj's is the second thing on my list of Things To Do With Roxanne in Paris.

"That sounds great," says Granny Bee. She yawns. "I'll freshen up, and then I'll help you in the kitchen."

Everybody was wrong about Roxanne. Everybody except me. Because all of us are cozy in the living room, wearing our pajamas and watching *Meet Me in St. Louis.* Just like in the old Three Rivers days.

And just like in Three Rivers, we both try to pretend we're not crying during the part when

Tootie runs outside. She smashes all of the snow people because she's sad and doesn't want to move away.

That part is especially sad this time because I remember how I felt when I didn't want to move away. Just like Tootie. But I didn't have any snow people lying around to smash. But now Roxanne is here, and she's the same Roxanne.

And Roxanne's pajamas are the ones that have dogs wearing wigs all over them. And she brought her old teddy bear, Osito, just like I knew she would.

Roxanne's ears are different, but everything else is the exact same. And that means this Christmas vacation is going to go exactly the way I planned.

Three

Mirabel Plouffe is always early. Sometimes this is annoying, like when I tell her to come over to my apartment for breakfast so she can meet Roxanne. She shows up at 7:30 a.m., which is too early for breakfast. It's too early for me to even be awake. Especially during school vacation.

I am still in bed with my puffy blue comforter pulled up to my ears. Roxanne is supposed to be sleeping on my trundle bed. But I hear lots of whispering, so I roll over and look. Roxanne isn't sleeping. She's sitting on top of the trundle next to Mirabel Plouffe. My two best friends in the whole world are meeting each other! And I'm missing it. I sit up.

"Winicker!" says Mirabel Plouffe. "I am sorry to be early. But I was so looking forward to meeting your friend!"

"Roxanne, this is Mirabel Plouffe," I say. I stretch my arms over my head and yawn. "Mirabel Plouffe, this is Roxanne."

"Bonjour again, Roxanne," says Mirabel Plouffe. She laughs.

"Bonjour again, Mirabel Plouffe," says Roxanne. "Ça va?"

Wait.

"Ça va bien," says Mirabel Plouffe.

What?

"Since when do you speak French?" I ask Roxanne.

She gives me a big smile. "Since I knew I was coming to visit you in Paris! I figured you probably speak a ton of French by now."

Mirabel Plouffe bursts out laughing. "Ho! Winicker! Speak French? I cannot even imagine it! When she must speak French in school, she says everything with such an American accent—"

"She does that when she tries Spanish, too!" Roxanne says, laughing.

"Anyway," I say. I do not like that Roxanne and Mirabel Plouffe are laughing about me. They are supposed to be laughing with me. They aren't the Tremendous Two. We're supposed to be the Tremendous Three.

Mirabel Plouffe pats a stripey red and white bag on the trundle next to her. "I brought le gui et le houx de Noël. These are Christmas plants French families sometimes hang above our doors at Christmastime. I thought Roxanne would like to see—"

"Roxanne would not like to see French Christmas plants," I say. "Roxanne would like to see the Christmas decorations we brought with us from Three Rivers. We're going to have a good old-fashioned Three Rivers Chr—"

"Actually," says Roxanne, "Miri's been telling me all about Christmas in Paris. It sounds awesome!"

"Miri?" I say. "It's Mirabel Plouffe. Everybody calls her Mirabel Plouffe." I yawn and get up.

"Well," says Mirabel Plouffe, "most people call me Mirabel. Just Mirabel."

"Okay," I say, "Let's just go decorate the apartment."

The grandmothers made breakfast. Grandma Balthazar's cinnamon rolls and Granny Bee's Chocolate de Agua. While we all eat together at the table, Mirabel Plouffe asks a million questions about the Chocolate de Agua. Mirabel Plouffe always asks a million questions about everything.

"C'est délicieux! This is what you drink in la République dominicaine?" Mirabel asks.

"Sí. I do not get to visit as much as I would like. But when I cook Dominican foods I feel like I am there," says Granny Bee.

Mirabel Plouffe takes a really deep breath and looks all dreamy. "I would love to visit one day. Is it very beautiful?"

"Oh, yes," says Granny Bee. She smiles. "There are miles and miles of beautiful beaches. The water is blue, the breeze is warm, and the coffee is delicioso."

"My mother loves coffee. And I want to see your blue water beaches someday," says Mirabel Plouffe. "What are the major exports of—"

"NO," I say. I do not want to hear about the major exports of anywhere. It is Christmas vacation, for Pete's sake.

Mirabel Plouffe looks disappointed. She eats a forkful of cinnamon roll.

"Roxanne," I say. "Mirabel Plouffe likes to read. Her mother works in a famous bookstore called Shakespeare and Company." Pretty soon, Roxanne and Mirabel will become very good friends and we will be the Tremendous Three.

"Oh yeah?" Roxanne says to Mirabel Plouffe. "That's cool. My friend Violet Kankiewicz's mother works at Amherst Books. Violet loves to read, too."

I get a bad feeling in my stomach. I know Violet Kankiewicz. Violet Kankiewicz isn't very interesting or fun. She's just fine.

She went to school with me and Roxanne ever since preschool. Sometimes, if we needed a third person to hold our jump rope, we asked Violet Kankiewicz. She was fine at holding the rope. She wasn't amazing. She didn't invent any new moves or tell any good jokes. And who cares if her mother works in a bookstore, anyway?

"I didn't know you and Violet were friends," I say to Roxanne. I take a sip of Chocolate de Agua like I don't care at all.

"Oh, yeah," says Roxanne. "She's one of my best friends now."

I get an even worse feeling in my stomach.

"Cool," I say, even though it isn't cool at all. "I thought she was best friends with Emmi and Maggie Wu."

Emmi and Maggie Wu are twins. They went to school with me and Roxanne ever since preschool, too. They are more interesting than Violet Kankiewicz, but only because they are twins. That is the most interesting thing about them. They don't even hold a jump rope very well.

"She is," says Roxanne. "We're all best friends. Me and Violet and Emmi and Maggie. It's kind of silly, but we call ourselves the Fabulous Four."

My mouth drops open, and my bite of cinnamon roll falls out.

"Winicker Wallace," says Grandma Balthazar. "Chew with your mouth closed!"

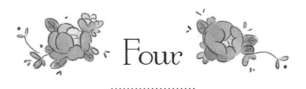

Four

So far, my day is not going the way I planned. Roxanne's whole visit isn't going the way I planned. When something goes wrong at Mom's work—if the wrong product gets delivered or the company sells more lipsticks than they have in stock—Mom rubs her forehead, takes a deep breath, and says, "Okay. Let's reset."

When something goes wrong with Dad's work—if his agent and his editor and Mom all tell him his new chapters aren't very good—he takes a deep breath too, and he says, "Okay. Starting over."

So that's what I do. I take a deep breath and I say, "Okay. Let's try again. How about we flock the windows?"

Mirabel Plouffe and Roxanne and I are all in the living room with a cardboard box that says Christmas Stuff on it in red Sharpie. The grown-ups said we can "deck the halls," which means we get to decorate the apartment. That is the fourth thing on my list of things to do with Roxanne.

"What do you mean, 'flock the windows?'" asks Mirabel Plouffe. "How do we 'flock the windows?'"

"We do it every year in Three Rivers," says Roxanne. "You take a can of flocking spray and spray the corners and bottoms of your windows to make it look like it snowed."

"Oh," says Mirabel Plouffe. "It does snow in Paris. Not very much, but it snows. Maybe we do not need to flock the windows?"

"We do," I say. I peel the tape off the top of the Christmas Stuff box and open it up. I dig around. All of our ornaments are wrapped up in bubble wrap. There's a tangled knot of fake cranberry garland and a couple of plastic candles. I pull those out.

"These go in the windows, too." I twist one of the flame-shaped bulbs on top of the candle. An orange light flickers on.

"I see," says Mirabel Plouffe.

I set down the candles on the coffee table. Then I move some packing paper in the box.

"Here it is!" I say. I pull out a silver can with snowflakes all over it and shake it up. "Who wants to do the flocking?"

"Let's let Miri do it," says Roxanne. "She's never done it before."

I feel kind of overheated and mad every time Roxanne calls Mirabel Plouffe "Miri," but I don't tell her that. Roxanne and Mirabel Plouffe are getting along really well, and we're on our way to being the Tremendous Three, which is much better than being the Fabulous Four.

"Good idea," I say.

All of a sudden, I hear Johnny Mathis singing "We Need A Little Christmas," and Dad pokes his head into the living room. "I thought you could use some holiday tunes while you get this place Christmas-ready," says Dad. "Grandma Balthazar and Granny Bee are baking cookies for you girls to decorate later."

"Thanks," I say. I feel a good kind of warm. There's Christmas music playing. The apartment smells like cookies baking. And I'm decorating for Christmas with my two best friends.

Mirabel Plouffe sprays the flocking spray onto one of the living room windows.

"Is this how it is supposed to look?" she asks.

"Whoa, Miri. That's really good," says Roxanne.

"Of course it is," I say. It looks perfect. Everything Mirabel Plouffe does looks perfect. Her school art projects. Her hair. Her face—well actually, her face looks kind of weird right now.

Pink patches with white bumps are spreading across her cheeks and chin and forehead.

"Mirabel Plouffe, are you okay?" I ask.

"Yeah, Miri, you've got a rash or something," says Roxanne.

Mirabel Plouffe touches her forehead. "I do feel strange," she says. "My face is very itchy."

She looks closely at the side of the flocking spray can. Then she sets down the can and backs away. "There are acrylates in that flocking spray."

"What are acrylates?" I ask.

"Do you need me to get Mr. Wallace?" says Roxanne. "Looking at your face is making me itchy."

"I am allergic to acrylates," says Mirabel Plouffe. She scratches one of her cheeks. "I should go home. I am sorry, Winicker and Roxanne, but I cannot help you decorate today." She scratches her other cheek.

"I'm sorry you're itchy, Mirabel Plouffe," I say. "I'll wash the flocking off that window so you can come over another day without being allergic." I look at the window. It's beautiful. I try not to seem too sad about having to wash it off.

"Rest up," says Roxanne. "I hope you can still come to the Christmas market with us tomorrow!"

Mirabel Plouffe smiles a little and scratches her chin. "I will feel better after a bath and a good night's sleep. Goodbye, Roxanne. Goodbye, Winicker. I will see you tomorrow."

Mirabel Plouffe picks up her stripey red bag and walks out of the living room. I can hear Grandma Balthazar and Granny Bee gasp in the kitchen.

". . . just an allergy," I hear Mirabel Plouffe saying. ". . . see you tomorrow."

It is a good thing Mirabel Plouffe lives next door. She would make a lot of people very nervous if she walked around like that.

"Man, Miri must be having a rough day," says Roxanne.

I feel kind of guilty about giving Mirabel Plouffe a rash. Really, though, who is allergic to acrylates? That's like being allergic to sheep. But I am glad she is going to come with us to the Christmas market on the Champs-Elysées.

I wipe the flocking spray off of the window and set up all of the fake flickery candles on the windowsills. Roxanne puts the Christmas pillows on the couch. One of the pillows is red with a gold reindeer on it. The other is gold with red letters that say "Ho! Ho! Ho!"

Granny Bee sticks her head into the living room. "Girls, the cookies are ready to decorate."

The cookies with the weird green frosting and silver balls! Roxanne and I have decorated these same cookies every single Christmas since we were four years old. It is a very special Christmas tradition. And I don't care what Maizy Durand says, they are the most delicious cookies in the whole world.

Except when we walk into the kitchen, our special tradition cookies aren't the cookies that are on the table. And there's no green frosting or silver balls! There's just seashell-shaped cookies and a bowl of melted chocolate.

"Voilà!" says Grandma Balthazar. She makes a sweeping gesture with her hand over the table.

"These look great!" says Roxanne.

"What are they?" I ask.

"They are Madeleine cookies," says Granny Bee. "Very French! You can dip them in chocolate and lay them out on this parchment paper until the chocolate sets."

"Miam!" says Roxanne.

"Miam indeed!" says Grandma Balthazar.

"NO," I say. My face and neck are hot, and I feel like a volcano that is about to erupt. "These are wrong! I don't want 'very French' cookies! I want the same old green cookies we make every single year!"

I look at Roxanne. "I thought this was going to be the best Christmas ever because my best friend was coming to visit. But it's the worst Christmas ever. You just want to do French stuff, and you don't care about any of our usual Christmas stuff."

"Winicker—" says Grandma Balthazar.

"No!" I say again. "Nobody even thinks about how I miss Three Rivers still. Or how my first Christmas in Paris is probably going to be hard. Nothing is the same as it was every other Christmas. I made a list, and I wanted to do the stuff on the list, but nobody cares!"

Roxanne's eyes are kind of watery, but I turn around and stomp to my room and shut the door. I get into bed and pull the covers up to my ears.

Normally when I'm very, very upset, I sit down at my desk and write a postcard to Roxanne. But this time, Roxanne is here. And she's the reason I'm upset. She has pierced ears, and she speaks French. She has all new friends, and she doesn't like doing the things we used to do together.

A warm tear rolls down my cheek and soaks into my pillow. She isn't the same old Roxanne at all.

At dinner on Sunday night, everyone sits around the kitchen table. Grandma Balthazar made asparagus risotto.

"This is wonderful, " says Granny Bee.

"Yeah," says Roxanne, "it's really good. I hope it's not too French for you, Winicker."

My face feels hot.

"I think risotto is Italian," says Dad, looking at his fork. "It sounds Italian. Isn't risotto Italian?"

"It's fine," I say to Roxanne.

"It's better than fine," Dad says to Grandma Balthazar. "You're a master of risotto."

"Girls," says Mom, looking back and forth between me and Roxanne. "Is everything okay?"

"I'm okay," says Roxanne. "I'm enjoying my once-in-a-lifetime trip to Paris. Trying to experience some French culture. Doing new things."

"I'm fine," I say, moving my risotto around the plate with my fork. "I just don't understand why somebody who is so obsessed with new things would even bother to visit her old friend. Personally, I like old things—no, traditional things. Some traditional things are great."

"I think the girls had different expectations for their visit," Grandma Balthazar says to Mom.

"Old things stink," says Roxanne. "Like old, stinky socks with holes in them. Or a rotten banana."

"New things stink!" I say. "Like green bananas. They're gross. And new shoes. They're not comfortable like a nice, familiar worn-in pair you've had forever and have wonderful memories with. New shoes don't even know you."

"Sometimes the old shoes don't fit anymore!" Roxanne shouts. For a second I think she's going to cry, but then she just looks angrier.

"I see," Mom says to Grandma Balthazar.

"I like new shoes," Dad says. "And old shoes. I like both." He looks down at his shoes.

"I think we could all use an early bedtime tonight," says Granny Bee. "I'm tired. You girls must be tired, too. Things always look brighter in the morning."

I am tired, actually. It was a long day. It started with a rash and ended with an awful fight with my best friend.

Roxanne looks at me and frowns. Then she looks at Granny Bee. "Granny Bee, can I sleep in Mr. Wallace's office with you tonight?"

Granny Bee does a big, sad sigh. "If you need to, honey. I don't think we're going to solve this tonight. But I hope you girls can work this out before we go to the Christmas market tomorrow."

"That's right," says Grandma Balthazar. "It's going to be a magical day. It would be such a shame for you not to enjoy it."

I go to my room and lay down on my bed. I try to be glad to have my room all to myself again. But I'm not glad at all.

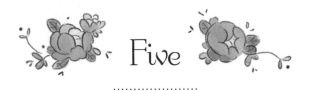

Five

There is only one bathroom in my apartment. And six people need to get ready to leave for the Christmas market. That means Roxanne and I don't have time to make up. But Grandma Balthazar said we're going anyway, so we go.

The Christmas market is very big and very busy. It is cold and a little rainy outside. We are all wearing sweaters under our raincoats. There are long rows of booths that look like little white houses. They are decorated with twinkle lights hanging like icicles and silver tinsel garland.

Mom, Dad, Grandma Balthazar, Granny Bee, Roxanne, Mirabel Plouffe, and I all crowd around a booth at the beginning of one of the rows. Dad is wearing Walter in a baby carrier on his chest.

Dad points to the giant Ferris wheel all the way at the end of the market.

"That's where we'll meet up again. The Ferris wheel at 3:00 p.m. Stay with your shopping buddies. My shopping buddies are your mom and Walter. Granny Bee is going to shop with Grandma Balthazar. Winicker, Roxanne, and Mirabel, you are going to walk around together. You girls have my phone. If you need us, you'll call your mom's phone. Is everybody ready?"

"Oui!" says Mirabel Plouffe. She looks around at everyone with a big smile on her face. Mirabel Plouffe always looks like somebody just offered her a giant ice cream sundae. She doesn't know Roxanne and I are fighting. "Is this Christmas market not the most charming thing in Paris?" She takes a deep breath through her nose.

Usually when Mirabel Plouffe takes a deep breath through her nose, it is annoying. She acts like the air smells like chocolate cake and evergreen trees, and it doesn't. But today the air really does smell like chocolate cake and evergreen trees. And cinnamon and oranges and roasted nuts.

All of the grown-ups leave. Mirabel Plouffe, Roxanne, and I follow our noses to a booth with shelves full of chocolate cakes shaped like logs.

"These smell great," says Roxanne. She leans forward and smells one of the chocolate logs.

Mirabel Plouffe nods. "La bûche de Noël. They are meant to look like logs. They taste wonderful!"

My stomach is grumbling. The little chalkboard on one of the shelves inside the booth says the chocolate logs are sixty euros each. That is a lot more than the twenty euros Mom and Dad gave me to spend at the Christmas market.

"Let's keep walking. I think they're selling roasted chestnuts in paper cones at that booth over there." I point to a booth farther down the row. There is a man in a white apron giving out samples.

We walk over to the booth and buy three cones of chestnuts. I crack one open and pop the inside into my mouth. It is warm and sweet and tastes exactly the way I thought it would. I close my eyes for a second.

"C'est délicieux," says Mirabel Plouffe.

I open one of my eyes and look at Roxanne. I wonder if she's going to talk to Mirabel Plouffe in French again. But she doesn't say anything. She just chews on her chestnut and looks down at her old boots like she's busy thinking.

We walk with our chestnut cones past a booth that sells all different kinds of cheese. Next, we pass another booth that sells little Christmas trees decorated with tiny bronze bells and red bows.

Then we see a booth that isn't selling anything at all. It is a nativity scene, but something is wrong. Everybody looks unhappy. There aren't three wise men. There are two. And every so often, the wise man in the red robe turns his head and gives a mean look to a guy who is drinking a cup of mulled cider at the booth next to the nativity.

The guy with the cup of cider is wearing a long orange robe and a crown with blue sparkly stones in it. It's the guy from the taxi!

"Hey," I say. "Remember me? You came to my apartment by accident a couple days ago."

The man scratches his beard. "Oh, yeah, I remember you!" He finishes his cider, tosses the paper cup into a nearby trash can, and sticks out his hand to us. "Charlie Baker, former wise man, recently unemployed. Are you enjoying the tableau vivant?"

"Oui," says Mirabel Plouffe. She shakes his hand excitedly and then clasps her hands together. "I love a good tableau vivant." That's really how she talks. "But are you supposed to be in it, Charlie? Why are there only two wise men?"

Charlie frowns. He looks at the wise man in the red robe and gives him a mean look right back. "That's a good question. Because the wise men are an important part of the nativity, right?"

Mirabel Plouffe nods. "Oh, yes. Very important."

"You can't really have a nativity scene with just two wise men, right?"

Mirabel Plouffe shakes her head dramatically. "Non! That would make no sense. There should be three."

"So if you had to choose between having a sheep in your nativity scene and having the third wise man, you would definitely choose to have the wise man, right?"

Mirabel Plouffe looks at the nativity scene again. She looks like she's thinking really hard about it, like it's a difficult homework problem. A woolly white sheep is lying on a pile of hay next to the cradle, snoring loudly.

"I do not know. I suppose the three wise men are more important than—"

"I hope you heard that, Barnard," Charlie yells to the grouchy wise man in the red robe. Barnard, I guess.

"Wait, are you fighting with one of the other wise men?" asks Roxanne. "This is the weirdest nativity I've ever seen. What happened?"

Charlie sighs and takes off his crown. "I'm allergic to the sheep. I took an allergy medicine this morning, and I'm still covered in hives. See?"

Charlie sticks out his arm and pulls up the sleeve of his robe. He has a big, bumpy rash on his arm. It looks like the rash Mirabel Plouffe got yesterday from the flocking spray.

"That looks pretty bad," says Roxanne. "So what's the problem? Why don't they just get a fake sheep and send this one home?"

"That's what I told them!" says Charlie. "But it's Barnard's sheep. He's very attached to it."

"No silly disagreement should come between friends," says Mirabel Plouffe. "There must be a way to work this out."

I look at Roxanne, but she's staring at her boots again.

"I don't see how," says Charlie. He throws his hands in the air. "I told Barnard I can't be around the sheep. He told me the sheep stays. 'It's traditional,' he says. What else is there for either of us to say?"

"Well," I say. "He might say it made him sad when you asked him to choose between him and the sheep. Especially since the sheep is so important to him. He probably planned on having his sheep in the tableau vivant all year long. It probably made him really sad when you told him he might have to change his plans."

Barnard walks up to us, nodding his head. "Oui! That is exactly how I felt. I felt sad. Molly goes everywhere with me. We do this together every year!"

"And you could probably tell Barnard it made you sad that he didn't listen to you when you needed him to replace his . . . Molly," says Roxanne, looking at Charlie. "It isn't like he has to give up his sheep forever. He just has to give it up for today. You could tell him that sometimes our friends are more important than traditions, even really good ones." She looks at me.

Charlie sticks his hands in the pockets of his orange robe and sniffs. He nods his head. "Barnard, I'm—"

"No," says Barnard. "I'm sorry."

The two wise men hug. The man who plays Joseph in the tableau vivant rolls his eyes and waves his staff at them both. "Now that everyone is friends again, can we get back to work?"

"Sure," says Barnard. "But first, I need to walk Molly home and get her settled with a snack."

Molly lifts her head up from the hay and yawns.

Roxanne, Mirabel Plouffe, and I throw away the paper cones from our roasted chestnuts.

"I didn't think about how this was an exciting new place for you. I didn't even ask you what you wanted to do. I let my plans get in the way of our friendship," I say to Roxanne.

"Hmm?" says Mirabel Plouffe.

"And I didn't think about how important traditions are to you. Especially when you're surrounded by all of this new stuff every day," says Roxanne. "I'm sorry, Winicker."

"I'm sorry, too," I say.

"What's that?" says Mirabel Plouffe.

Roxanne hugs me tight, and I hug her back. We both pull in Mirabel Plouffe, and all three of us laugh. My heart feels full of Three Rivers and Christmas, even if there aren't any green cookies or flocked windows around.

"We shouldn't feel too bad," Roxanne says. "Even wise men have this problem."

Then a familiar voice yells, "Winicker! Winicker Wallace! Mirabel! Over here!"

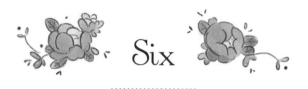

Six

MAKE A GINGERBREAD HOUSE

Mirabel Plouffe and I look around to find the person with the familiar voice. Then we spot her. Standing in a booth behind a counter full of gingerbread houses is Amal Aziz!

"Amal!" I yell. Roxanne, Mirabel Plouffe, and I run over to Amal's booth. A banner hanging under the counter says La Nourriture. The shelves behind Amal are full of beautiful, delicious gingerbread houses, too. Which is strange for a health food and vegan footwear booth.

Except it was only from far away that the gingerbread houses looked beautiful and delicious. Now that we're up close they still look beautiful, but they don't look delicious at all. The walls aren't made out of gingerbread. They're made out of crackers with seeds in them. And it looks like everything is held together with some kind of brown goo instead of frosting.

"Is that peanut butter?" I ask Amal.

A woman standing behind Amal smiles at me. She is wearing a long coat with pink and blue roses all over it and shiny leggings. "This is sunflower butter," the woman says. "It is just as delicious as peanut butter. Very high in protein and not as processed as most peanut butter."

I doubt sunflower butter is as delicious as peanut butter. A fluffernutter sandwich made with sunflower butter is probably gross. And I know sunflower butter isn't as delicious as frosting. I wonder what a fluffernutter sandwich with frosting would taste like.

The woman holds her hand out to me. "I am Amal's mother. Please, call me Kadijah."

I shake her hand. Mirabel Plouffe and Roxanne shake her hand, too. Kadijah's nails are very fancy. They are pink with gold glitter on the tips.

"I like your nail polish," I say.

"Thank you," says Kadijah. "These are vegan, eco-friendly nail polishes."

"Cool," says Roxanne.

"Très chic," says Mirabel Plouffe.

"And I like your silver hair," says Kadijah.

I pat my hair. "Thank you," I say. "I'm not sure if it's vegan."

Kadijah laughs.

None of these cracker houses have candy on them. Some of them have dried orange slices for the windows and roofs made out of lots of tiny almond slices. They all have yards full of shredded coconut snow. There are pecan doors and cranberry ornaments on the little wreaths hanging on most of the houses.

I lean forward and sniff one of the wreaths. It smells like soup and soap.

"What's this made out of?" I ask.

"The wreath? It is made out of sprigs of rosemary," says Kadijah. "Amal made them. And she designed these beautiful houses! Isn't she talented?"

"Oui, Amal is very talented," says Mirabel Plouffe. "C'est une artiste."

"Nice job, Amal," I say, even though the rosemary wreath smells weird. But Amal isn't paying attention. She is looking at something. We all turn our heads to look, too.

There is a bicycle riding slowly, pulling a delicious-looking cart of pastries. The woman riding the bicycle waves at us. She is wearing an old-fashioned dress and a wide-brimmed black hat that keeps the rain out of her face. There are tiny silver Eiffel Tower earrings in her ears. The banner on the side of her cart says Sweet Spoken.

"That bicycle patisserie sells its pastries, crafts, and jewelry near La Nourriture," says Kadijah. "That woman is Emily-the-Bicycle-Woman. She is an American like you, Winicker. She's lovely. "

Amal's family probably doesn't mind that Emily-the-Bicycle-Woman sets up near them.

Nobody shopping for a cracker house would accidentally buy delicious pastries instead.

"I love her earrings," says Roxanne.

"Les macarons look wonderful," says Amal. She looks hungry and far away.

"I have to ask her something. Hold on a minute," I say. I run up to Emily-the-Bicycle-Woman. I make sure I stand so my friends can't see what I buy from her.

When I am finished shopping from the Sweet Spoken bicycle cart, I return to Amal's booth. I am now carrying a small white paper bag. Mirabel Plouffe and Roxanne look very curious about what I bought.

"It's a Christmas secret," I say.

Amal looks curious at first. But she sniffs my bag and loses interest. Now she is sniffing the air.

"I smell chocolate," she says. "And cream puffs. I smell a tower of cream puffs covered in chocolate."

I sniff the air, too. It smells sweet, but I couldn't guess what kind of sweet.

"Wow! That's a pretty great talent, identifying yummy smells. I'm Roxanne," says Roxanne. She sounds impressed. "Let's go find some cream puffs."

"I am Amal," says Amal. "It is wonderful to meet you. I think the smell is coming from that direction." Amal points toward the Ferris wheel. She looks at her mother. "May I go with them?"

Kadijah wrinkles her nose. "I need your help selling these gingerbread houses today, Amal. And cream puffs are full of sugar!" Kadijah rummages through her purse. She pulls out a small cloth bag and an orange. "If you want a snack, I packed raw cashews and oranges! Much less sugar than cream puffs, and just as delicious!"

Cashews and oranges are definitely not as delicious as cream puffs. Amal makes a sad face at us.

"Enjoy your cream puffs," she says. "It was nice to meet you, Roxanne."

"Enjoy your cashews," I say. Mirabel Plouffe, Roxanne, and I wave at Amal. We walk toward the smell.

"It is no wonder Amal draws pictures of cookies and cakes on all of her homework," says Mirabel Plouffe.

"Poor Amal," says Roxanne.

"Poor Amal," Mirabel Plouffe and I say at the same time.

"Her mom does have really nice nails, though," says Roxanne.

The booth with the chocolate-covered cream puffs is more beautiful than anything I have ever seen. It is even more beautiful than Amal's cracker houses. There are hills of cream puffs on gold paper doilies. Some of them are dripping with chocolate. Some have snowy powdered sugar all over them. And others are covered in a web of golden spun sugar.

"I feel really bad for Amal now," I say.

"I feel even worse for us," says Roxanne. She points to the chalkboard with the prices written on it. Seventy euros! That is even more than the chocolate logs! And after what I bought from Emily-the-Bicycle-Woman, I am out of money.

"Oh, my stomach," says Mirabel Plouffe. "The smell is making me so hungry!"

"Me too," I say.

And then I smell something very familiar. I smell cookies with green frosting and silver balls! Well, I don't smell the frosting or the balls. But I smell the cookies! Christmas cookies! The kind we always made in Three Rivers. I am not as gifted as Amal about identifying smells. But I'd know that smell anywhere.

I take a deep breath. "Roxanne, do you smell that?" I ask.

Roxanne closes her eyes. "Look, I know what I said about wanting to eat French stuff while I'm here. And I still do. But right now I am so hungry. Those Three Rivers-smelling cookies have got to cost less than seventy euros."

"Oh yes," says Mirabel Plouffe. "They smell wonderful. I think the smell is coming from this booth over here."

We follow Mirabel Plouffe to a booth that reminds me so much of Three Rivers, it gives me a pain in my heart. There is a plate of Christmas cookies on the counter. Real Three Rivers Christmas cookies with green frosting and silver balls on them! There is a small forest of tall tinselly candy canes in the back of the booth. There is a sleigh attached to eight reindeer strung from fishing line. It looks like it is flying over the candy canes.

There is also a large model of a shiny boat on the counter. The boat is decorated with a string of tiny red and green Christmas lights. Stacks of brochures with pictures of a real boat on them surround the model. "Deck the Halls" is playing on a stereo in the back of the booth.

"Well hello, ladies," says a man. The man has an American accent! "Help yourself to a cookie."

Mirabel Plouffe, Roxanne, and I each take a cookie. I take a big bite of mine.

"This tastes exactly like Three Rivers," I say through my mouthful of cookie.

"Well now, you can't be talking about Three Rivers, Massachusetts, can you?" asks the man.

"Whoa! You know Three Rivers?" asks Roxanne. "That's where we're from!"

The man shakes his head and holds his belly and chuckles. "I sure do know Three Rivers," he says. "I'm from Ware, Massachusetts! That's just a couple of minutes away!"

"Ware! My dentist was in Ware," I say.

"It's very nice to meet you girls! I'm Mr. Socha. I'll tell you what. Just for my new Massachusetts friends, I'll give you a discount on our very famous Tour of Lights on the Seine."

The man waves his hand over the model boat with the Christmas lights on it. "How would you like to take your parents on a magical Christmas Eve boat ride on the world's most famous river tomorrow night? How would you like to truly experience the Christmas season? Traditional caroling and a dazzling light display. Plus, a tour of all of the most famous landmarks in the City of Love. These include the Eiffel Tower, Notre Dame, and the Colosseum, of course."

Roxanne and I raise our eyebrows at each other. The Tour of Lights on the Seine sounds perfect! Roxanne can see all the parts of Paris she wants to see. And there will be Christmas caroling and lights for me, too!

"Will there be more of these cookies?" I ask.

The man chuckles again. "Of course there will!"

"Well then," I say, "I'm going to call my mom. The grown-ups are going to love this idea!" I take out Dad's phone and call Mom.

"That is strange," Mirabel Plouffe says quietly. "The Colosseum is in Rome. It cannot be seen from la Seine."

Mirabel Plouffe always turns everything fun into a geography lesson.

"Wait, did he say the City of Love?" asks Roxanne.

"Mom," I say into the phone. "Come meet us. Roxanne and I have the best idea!"

Seven

LOOK AT CHRISTMAS LIGHTS

It is Christmas Eve! For the first time since Roxanne got here, everything is going exactly right! We are all dressed up and ready to board the cruise ship and take the magnificent Tour of Lights on the Seine.

Except for baby Walter and Dad. Babies aren't allowed on the Tour of Lights. And babies can't stay home alone. I asked. So Dad is staying home with Walter. Dad gets seasick anyway.

Mirabel Plouffe can't come, either. Her family eats oysters for dinner and goes to midnight mass every Christmas Eve.

Grandma Balthazar and Granny Bee look more glamorous than ever. They are wearing long, belted coats and shimmery scarves. Mom is wearing her fancy, white wool coat and a cranberry-colored scarf that matches her pants.

Roxanne and I are wearing our brand-new Christmas pajamas under our coats. It's just like when we used to drive around to look at Christmas lights in Three Rivers. My Christmas pajamas have little Santa faces wearing heart-shaped glasses. Roxanne's have gingerbread men on skateboards.

Mr. Socha appears in front of the boat. "Welcome, " he says to us and the twenty people around us. "Are you ready to see some sights?"

Everyone at the dock looks around at each other. "Yes!" a few people yell. A couple of people clap their hands, but not very loudly.

"I can't hear you! Are you ready to see some spectacular Christmas lights?" Mr. Socha yells.

"Yes!" More people yell this time.

"Then board our beautiful tour boat, and let's go!" yells Mr. Socha.

Families begin boarding the boat. There is a lot of very excited whispering and a little bit of confused murmuring.

The tour boat looks like a long bus with a lot of seats and no roof, except where the steering wheel is. It definitely doesn't look like the beautiful ship on Mr. Socha's counter, but I don't mind. I bet it will look much better when they turn on the lights and the music!

"Merry Christmas," Mr. Socha greets each passenger that climbs onto the boat. "Merry Christmas. And Merry Christmas to you!"

It's finally our turn to climb onto the boat. "Mr. Socha, do you remember us?" I ask.

"Of course!" says Mr. Socha. "How could I forget the girls from Michigan City, Indiana? Practically my hometown!"

"Wait," says Roxanne. "We're not from—"

"Hurry, hurry, hurry," says Mr. Socha. "Get yourselves a seat! It's almost time!"

"Time for what?" I ask, but Mr. Socha is already talking to the man with his two sons behind us.

"Ah, there are my boys from Issaquah, Washington," says Mr. Socha. "Just a few minutes away from Bellevue, where I'm from!"

"He said he was from Ware," I say to Roxanne. We sit down on our wooden bench seats.

Roxanne shrugs. "Maybe he moved a lot?"

A woman with big maroon hair and a very puffy fur coat stands up at the front of the boat. She turns to face everyone. "Hello hello," she says. She wraps her arms around her fur like she's giving herself a hug. "Merry Christmas, friends! I'm Mrs. Socha. Mr. Socha and I are thrilled to spend Christmas Eve with you. Very soon, we will begin our tour. Before our departure, who would like some Christmas treats?"

All of the kids and some of the grown-ups raise their hands in the air. Mr. Socha walks around with a tray full of little paper plates with green frosted cookies. I shiver a little, both because it's very cold on the Seine and because it feels just exactly like Christmas. Sitting with Roxanne and Grandma Balthazar and Granny Bee and Mom. Waiting to see the lights and eat Christmas cookies and listen to Christmas music.

"And who would like some of my famous holiday punch?" says Mrs. Socha.

Everyone raises their hands. Mr. Socha walks around with a tray full of paper cups. He looks at his big gold watch every couple of seconds. Roxanne and Granny Bee and Grandma Balthazar and Mom and I all take a cup.

I take a sip. The punch doesn't taste like punch. The punch doesn't have a color. There are two cranberries floating in it.

Mom makes a face after taking a sip of her punch. "I think this is just seltzer water with cranberries in it," she says.

"Mine is seltzer water, too, but it doesn't have cranberries in it," says Grandma Balthazar. She reaches inside her cup and pulls out a cinnamon stick.

"Gross," says Roxanne.

We all hold our cups in our laps politely.

"The cookies are good, though!" I say.

The boat jolts.

"Is everybody ready?" yells Mr. Socha.

"Yes!" the whole group yells back this time.

"Then here we go!" Mr. Socha waves at whoever is steering the boat up on the covered platform behind us.

We pull away from the dock.

"I wonder when they're going to turn on the lights?" I whisper to Roxanne.

Mr. Socha stands up in front of everyone. He isn't holding a tray anymore.

"Do you see that over there?" He points to something far away to our left. We all stretch our

necks out to look. "That is the Arc de Brioche. Very famous. Very, very French."

"I don't see anything," whispers Granny Bee.

"What is the Arc de Brioche? It isn't in my book," whispers Roxanne.

"Brioche is a pastry. Does he mean the Arc de Triomphe?" says Grandma Balthazar.

"The Arc de Triomphe isn't over there," says Mom.

"And right there, big as a mountain, you can see the Eiffel Tower! Also very famous and French," says Mr. Socha. He scratches his neck.

"That actually is the Eiffel Tower, thankfully," says Grandma Balthazar.

The Eiffel Tower is beautiful. It twinkles in the night like a giant Christmas tree.

"But wait! What's that I see? It's the reason we call this the Tour of Lights!" Mr. Socha points to a double-decker tour boat in the distance. It is all lit up. Its sparkling white lights reflect in the water. It is much nicer than our boat.

"Ooooh," says Mrs. Socha. She motions for us all to join her.

"Ooooh," a few people say. But no one sounds very excited. Nobody claps. A lot of people are crossing their arms and shaking their heads.

Where are the lights on our tour boat?

"We're going to try to get closer to that boat over there. But sometimes they get a little cranky. Everyone, relax and have fun. Enjoy making all of these Christmas memories. If you listen really, really closely, you can even hear the music playing on that boat. Try to guess the song! It's like a game!"

I put my hand up to my ear and listen closely. I don't hear any music. All I hear is a bunch of angry muttering. What a weird game.

Eight

LISTEN TO CHRISTMAS MUSIC

"**W**inicker," says Roxanne. "I think we've been scammed."

We look at each other for a second. Then we burst out laughing.

"What is so funny, girls?" asks Granny Bee. "Is this the whole tour? We're just going to follow that other boat around?"

"Yes!" I say. I am laughing so hard I have to hold onto my stomach.

"Arc de Brioche!" says Roxanne. She holds onto my shoulder and laughs so hard I think we're both going to fall over.

"This is ridiculous!" Mom says to Grandma Balthazar. "What a strange way to spend Christmas Eve."

They shake their heads at each other. But they are both smiling just a tiny bit.

"Ho ho ho! Does anybody hear that?" Mr. Socha has to cup his hands over his mouth to talk over everyone.

The boat gets quiet. I don't hear anything.

"Could that be Peter Noël I hear?" says Mr. Socha.

"Who is Peter Noël?" asks Roxanne.

"I think he means Père Noël," says Grandma Balthazar. "Father Christmas."

All of the people on the boat whisper to each other. Then I do hear something.

"Ho ho ho!"

Everyone looks around. A man in a long, red cloak appears in the doorway of the covered platform where the steering wheel is. He waves at us and climbs down to the deck.

"Ho ho ho!" he says again. "Take off your shoes!"

Everyone whispers again.

"Who is driving the boat?" somebody yells over the whispers.

"What? Take off my shoes?" Mom says. She looks down at her shoes. They are suede, gold, and lacy, with pointy toes and a very tall heel. I heard Dad say they cost more than his first car.

"Take off your shoes, children!" says the man in the red cloak. "Because if you have been good, I will fill your shoes with candy!"

Mom crosses her ankles and tucks her gold, lacy high-heeled feet under the bench.

I shrug at Roxanne and take off my shoes. She does, too. Candy is candy.

"Take off your shoes, moms and dads, grandmothers and grandfathers," says the man in the red cloak. "If you have been good, I will fill your shoes with candy, too!"

"You heard him," says Mr. Socha. "Take off your shoes for Peter Noël!"

"Père Noël," Grandma Balthazar says, loud enough for the people around us to hear. "He means Père Noël." She looks at her feet. She is wearing copper-colored shoes that look like slippers a princess would wear. "Why not?" she says. She slides out of her shoes.

Granny Bee does the same thing. Her shoes look like fuzzy red ballet slippers. "You're only young once," she says. She and Grandma Balthazar laugh.

Peter Noël walks around filling everyone's shoes with handfuls of candy. Everyone's shoes except Mom's, who is hiding hers under the bench.

After Peter Noël gets to our bench, I pick up my shoes to see what kind of candy is in there.

"Oh, gross," says Roxanne. She is looking inside her shoes, too. "He put gumdrops in here. Like, naked gumdrops. Now they're going to taste like foot sweat."

I got gumdrops, too. And a couple pieces of licorice. I pop one of the gumdrops into my mouth. Then I spit it out into my hand.

"Foot sweat?" says Roxanne.

"I wish it tasted like foot sweat," I say. "It's the kind of gumdrop that don't taste like a flavor. It just tastes spicy."

I look around for a trash can. I don't see one.

"What are we supposed to do with this candy?" I ask Mom. "How do we put our shoes back on when they're full of naked candy?"

"Here," says Grandma Balthazar. She opens her big purse. "You can shake your shoes out in here."

I reach for my shoes. I hear something rumble.

"Oh, snap," says Roxanne.

Buckets of water start pouring from the sky. We are getting soaked! There is no roof, and nothing to hide under! Grandma Balthazar and Granny Bee hold their purses over their heads.

Mom tucks her purse under the bench next to her shoes, because it's expensive. I heard Dad say it cost more than his first apartment. Mom sits quietly on the bench with her eyes closed.

"Winicker, our shoes!" says Roxanne.

By the time I pick mine up, they are already filled with orangey-black goo.

"Oh, gross," I say. "These are my favorite shoes, too!"

"My beautiful mules!" says Grandma Balthazar. She shakes the wet candy goop out of her shoe and into her hand. She looks around to see what everyone else is doing with theirs. Everyone else looks just as confused. Almost everyone on the deck has a dripping handful of orange and black candy.

"My ballet flats," says Granny Bee. "My brand-new flats." She shakes her head and whacks the bottom of her shoes to get all of the candy out.

Beeeep.

Everyone looks around to see where the sound is coming from.

Beeeep.

Mr. Socha, Mrs. Socha, and Peter Noël are all crowded in the little room with the steering wheel. And the only roof on the boat.

Beeep.

Mr. Socha is pressing the button on the intercom.

"Oh boy, it's really raining, folks!" says Mr. Socha. "I'm sorry about that. I'm sure it'll stop soon. But until it does, let's sing some Christmas carols. Here, Peter, why don't you take over? How about some 'Deck the Halls?'"

Peter Noël squishes past Mr. and Mrs. Socha to get to the intercom.

"Deck the Halls with hmm hmm holly, fa la la la la la la la la."

"Did he just say 'hmm hmm holly?'" Grandma Balthazar says from under her purse.

"Hmm hmm season to be jolly, fa la la la la la la la la," sings Peter Noël.

"Somebody needs to give Peter Noël a sheet of lyrics," says Mom.

"Don we now hmm hmm hmm hmm hmm, fa la la la la la la la la. Troll the hoo dee doo be doo bah, fa la la la la la la la la."

Everyone on the deck is soaking wet and roaring with laughter.

"This is some Christmas Eve!" says Mom. She laughs and wipes some runny mascara from under her eyes. "I can't believe your dad is missing this! He is going to be so disappointed!"

When we are finally docked again, the rain has stopped. We all file off the boat. Mr. and Mrs. Socha stand at the exit saying goodbye. When we reach them, Mr. Socha nods at us.

"My favorite girls from Litchfield, New Hampshire," he says. "You know, it's customary to tip in Paris." He wiggles his eyebrows.

"Here you go," I say. I shove both of my shoes full of gooey candy into his open hands.

"Merry Christmas, Mr. Socha," says Roxanne. We jump onto the dock squealing with laughter. My feet are bare and cold, but my cheeks are warm.

Nine

When we are home and dry, Roxanne and I curl up on the couch. We are now in fresh, dry, non-Christmas pajamas.

"It's late, girls," says Mom. "Make sure you get to bed before too long. If you don't go to bed, Peter Noël won't come." She laughs and laughs.

"Goodnight, Winicker," says Dad. "Goodnight, Roxanne." As he walks away, I hear him mutter, "I can't believe I missed it. What a night!"

Grandma Balthazar turned on the Yule log video we brought with us from Three Rivers. Roxanne and I are pretending it's a real fire. The Yule log reminds me of the Yule log cakes at the Christmas market. And that reminds me I have the best Christmas present for Roxanne.

"Can we do presents tonight instead of in the morning?" I ask.

"Uh, sure," says Roxanne. "The problem is, yours isn't arriving until tomorrow." She makes a guilty kind of face.

"That's okay! I have yours in my room. I'll go get it."

I go to my room and rummage around in my desk drawer. I find the white paper bag that I bought from Emily-the-Bicycle-Woman at the Christmas market. I open the bag and take out a little pink box. I squeeze the box in my hand and close my eyes. I hope Roxanne loves it. I think she's going to love it.

When I get back to the couch, I hand Roxanne the little pink box.

She opens the box, and her eyes get full of tears. She pulls out the earrings. They are tiny silver Eiffel Towers. They are just like the ones I saw in Emily-the-Bicycle-Woman's ears. When I

asked the Bicycle Woman, she told me she sells them. So I bought a pair for Roxanne.

"Winicker. This is the best present I have ever gotten." Roxanne takes her gold earrings out and puts them in the little pink box. Then she puts the silver Eiffel Tower earrings in her earlobes. "You are the best friend ever."

"So are you," I say.

And even though it didn't seem like it at first, this Christmas is the best. And this visit is the best. And this—

Roxanne lets out a very loud, very long snore. She's asleep! She's asleep on the couch in front of the fake Yule log.

I sneak out of the living room and into my bedroom. I'm tired, too, but there's something I want to do before I go to sleep. I sit down at my desk. I take a new postcard out of my desk drawer and start writing.

Dear Roxanne,

You are still at my apartment, but you will be back at your house by the time this postcard gets to Three Rivers. I am glad you are my friend. And I am glad you came to spend Christmas with me. I am also glad we got to take the magnificent Tour of Lights together. I hope Granny Bee's ballet flats are dry by the time you read this.

I miss you already.

Love,

Winicker

I don't think very many people have two best friends, but I'm glad I do. Even though one of them is allergic to flocking spray. And the other thinks Violet Kankiewicz is an actual fun person now. My best friendness with Mirabel Plouffe doesn't mean my best friendness with Roxanne is any smaller than it used to be.

So I am okay with Roxanne being the Fabulous Four with Violet and Emmi and Maggie. Because she is still the Terrific Two with me. And the Tremendous Three with me and Mirabel Plouffe. And the—well, we probably don't need to keep coming up with names for it. We're best friends. And that is enough.

Ten

It is Christmas morning, and everyone is here! Mom and Dad and Walter and Grandma Balthazar and Granny Bee and Roxanne and Mirabel Plouffe and Mrs. Plouffe. We are all eating Grandma Balthazar's famous crepes. Well, all except Walter. He is too little for crepes. Mom is giving him a bottle instead.

And actually, they are not Grandma Balthazar's famous crepes. They are Julia Child's famous crepes. I know this because Grandma Balthazar left her Julia Child cookbook open to the crepe page on the counter. And before she went shopping yesterday, she wrote down all of the ingredients from that crepe page in Julia Child's cookbook. But I don't tell anyone.

"Mmm," says Mirabel Plouffe. "Grandma Balthazar, your cooking is wonderful."

"Thank you, Mirabel," says Grandma Balthazar. "What a lovely thing to say!"

Mirabel Plouffe always says lovely things. She is a lovely person. I'm glad she is my FBFANDN. That reminds me!

"Mirabel Plouffe, I have a present for you!" I say.

Mirabel Plouffe looks very surprised. She looks like she has never received a present before in her whole life. Which is not true, obviously. She fans herself with her hand.

"Oh, Winicker, thank you! And I have a present for you, also. But it will arrive at your door in twenty minutes."

"What a coincidence," says Roxanne. She winks at Mirabel Plouffe, like they both know something I don't know. "My gift for you is going to be here in twenty minutes, too, Winicker!"

Mirabel Plouffe smiles at Roxanne. "We have good taste!"

We finish our crepes, and Mirabel Plouffe follows me into my room. I pull her present out of my desk drawer. It is flat and square and wrapped in red paper. I tied a gold ribbon around it. I tried to make a bow on top, but I made a really tight knot instead.

"Joyeux Noël, Mirabel Plouffe," I say. I hand her the present.

"Merry Christmas, Winicker," says Mirabel Plouffe.

She unwraps the present as carefully as if she is giving a baby bird a tiny sponge bath. I try not to make an impatient face.

When she is finished removing the paper, she shrieks. "Winicker Wallace! You are the most thoughtful—I cannot—I love this gift with all of my heart!" Mirabel Plouffe's face is very pink. Her smile is so big I wonder if her face hurts.

She holds up the gift. It is a picture of the two of us that Grandma Balthazar took when we all went to the Latin Quarter together. We are sharing a crepe, and we have chocolate smeared on our faces. Strings of lights hang above our heads. People are dancing behind us. I wrote FBFANDN in gold marker on the purple frame. She hugs the picture to her chest.

"You are my FBFANDN too, Winicker." Mirabel Plouffe looks like she might cry. I hope she doesn't.

Knock knock.

Someone is at the door.

Mirabel Plouffe looks at the small silver watch around her wrist. "It is here!" she says. "Your gift is here!"

We rush to the kitchen. When I open the door, Amal Aziz is standing there with two boxes in her arms. Her mother is standing behind her.

"Hi, Amal! Hi, Kadijah!" I say.

"Hello, girls," says Kadijah. "We have two very special packages for Winicker."

Mirabel Plouffe takes the box on top from Amal and brings it over to the table. I take the second box.

"Thanks, Amal," I say. "Do you want to come in?"

"We'd love to, but we have more deliveries to make. Happy holidays to your families, girls," says Kadijah.

"See you in school!" says Amal.

When Amal and her mother leave, I put the second box on the table. Both boxes say *To Winicker,* but one says *From Roxanne.* The other says *From Mirabel Plouffe.*

I unwrap the present from Mirabel Plouffe first. She is smiling really big and wiggling around in her chair. I can tell she is really excited for me to open it.

"I am sorry I did not wrap it myself. Usually I make my own paper with stamps I carve from potatoes," says Mirabel Plouffe. Of course she carves stamps out of potatoes.

When the box is unwrapped, I lift the top off and peer inside. It looks like a roof made out of a billion almond slivers. Mirabel Plouffe claps her hands.

"I saw how much you loved these at the Christmas market," she says. "And, as you know, the lavender flowers in the little window boxes are one of France's agricultural exports!"

Mirabel Plouffe got me a cracker house. And a French economics lesson.

"Wow, Mirabel Plouffe," I say. "Thank you!"

I lift the cracker house out of the box. Mirabel Plouffe is practically glowing. I sniff it. It still smells like soup and soap.

"Merry Christmas, Winicker!" says Mirabel Plouffe.

"Merry Christmas, Mirabel Plouffe," I say. I give her a big hug. Because even though I do not plan to eat the cracker house, it really is beautiful. And Mirabel Plouffe really is my FBFANDN.

"My turn," says Roxanne. She nudges the smaller box toward me.

I unwrap it and lift off the top. I hope it's not another cracker house.

Inside the box is the most awesome pair of mermaid-sequined shoes I have ever seen.

"Roxanne!" I say. I take them out of the box. They sparkle like Paris and silver hair and the Eiffel Tower at night. "These are amazing! These are perfect!"

"I hoped you'd like them! Apparently they're vegan. If you wanted to eat them," says Roxanne. "I'm writing you a poem, too, but it isn't done yet."

I slide my new shoes onto my feet. They fit perfectly. "I love them!" I say. "New shoes are the best."

Roxanne gets up from her chair and gives me a big, squeezy hug.

"Old shoes are pretty great, too," she says. "When they're not full of candy goop."

'TWAS THE NIGHT BEFORE CHRISTMAS
A VISIT FROM ROXANNE

BY ROXANNE RODRIGUEZ

'Twas the night before Christmas
and out on the boat
we didn't see lights
and we needed raincoats.

The cookies were good
but the sights were not.
The Tour of Lights wasn't worth
the tickets we bought.

The Arc de Brioche
was not to be seen,
because it doesn't exist.
It never has been.

Peter Noël filled our shoes
with really gross candy.
We wished there had been
a wastebasket handy.

But the evening itself
was not really that bad.
It was probably the funniest
Christmas Eve I have had.

And after my visit
has come to an end,
I'll remember the Tour
that I shared with my friend.

Winicker Wallace's

Bonjour: Good day

Brioche: A sweet French bread

Ça va?: How's it going?

Ça va bien: It's going well.

C'est délicieux: It is delicious.

C'est une artiste: She is an artist.

Chocolate de Agua: (Spanish) A Dominican cinnamony hot chocolate drink

Delicioso: (Spanish) Delicious

Derrière: Butt

El bebé: (Spanish) The baby

Ho!: Oh!

La bûche de Noël: A Christmas cake shaped like a log

Le gui et le houx de Noël: Mistletoe and Holly

Joyeux Noël: Merry Christmas

Merci: Thank you

Miam: Yum

La Petite École Internationale de Paris: The Little International School of Paris

La Nourriture: Food

La République dominicaine: The Dominican Republic

Les Macarons: Very tasty cookies

Non!: No!

Osito: (Spanish) Little bear

Oui: Yes

Parisien: Parisian

Père Noël: Father Christmas

Sablés: Buttery French cookies

Sí: (Spanish) Yes

Tableau vivant: A group of people arranged in a scene

Très chic: Very stylish

Voici: Here it is

Voilà: There it is

Meet the Author

Renee Beauregard Lute lives in the Pacific Northwest with one husband, two cats, and three amazing children. (Maddie, Simon, and Cecily, that's you!) There are many writers in the Pacific Northwest, and Renee is one of them. There may also be sasquatches in the Pacific Northwest, but Renee is not a sasquatch.

Like Winicker, Renee is from Western Massachusetts and loves macarons and sending postcards. Unlike Winicker, Renee has never lived in Paris, but she is very certain she would not hate it, even if Mirabel Plouffe lived next door.

Meet the Illustrator

Laura K. Horton is a freelance illustrator that has always had a passion for family, creativity and imagination. She earned her BFA in illustration and animation from the Milwaukee Institute of Art and Design. When she's not working, she can be found drinking tea, reading, and game designing. Recently she has moved to Espoo, Finland, to obtain a masters degree in game design and development.